PUBLISHER'S NOTE:

Since its publication in 1915, Robert Frost's "The Road Not Taken" has become one of the world's most oft-quoted poems. Though originally meant by Frost as a joke about indecisiveness, the poem has since been adopted by many as a call to individualism and adventure. In this book, we present a gentle homage to both possibilities—indeed, to both roads. Some scenes capture the difficulty of decision. Some celebrate the magic of serendipity. And some raise an insolvable question: does happiness come from making the right choices at all, or from simply finding joy in whatever journey we find ourselves on?

We can't say where these questions and roads will lead, and so we invite you, dear reader, to step into the yellow wood. There, may you reflect on *your* road and, in so doing, find joy and inspiration and discover for yourself what might make "all the difference."

Your journey awaits . . .

To my parents, Debbie and Sam, who showed me how to
keep my head up and keep going forward. —V. M.

FAMILIUS

Text originally published by Robert Frost in *The Atlantic Monthly* in 1915 and later in *Mountain Interval* in 1916.
Illustration copyright © 2019 by Vivian Mineker.
All rights reserved.

Published by Familius LLC.
PO Box 1249 Reedley, Ca 93654.
www.familius.com

Library of Congress Cataloging-in-Publication Data

2018956352   ISBN 9781641701075   eISBN 9781641701358

Book and jacket design by David Miles

Printed in China

10 9 8 7 6

First Edition

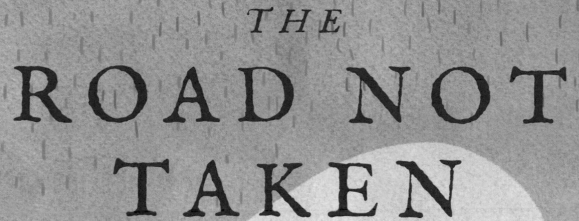

THE
ROAD NOT
TAKEN

ROBERT FROST

With illustrations by
VIVIAN MINEKER

Two roads diverged in a yellow wood,

And sorry I could not travel both
And be one traveler,

long I stood

And looked down one as far as I could
To where it bent in the undergrowth;

Then took the other,
as just as fair,

And having perhaps the better claim,
Because it was grassy and wanted wear;

Though as for that the passing there
Had worn them really about the same,

And both that morning equally lay

In leaves no step had
trodden black.

Oh, I kept the first
for another day!

Yet knowing how way

leads on to way,

I doubted if I should ever come back.

I shall be telling this with a sigh
Somewhere ages and ages hence:

Two roads
diverged in a
wood, and I—

I took the one less traveled by,

And that has made all the difference.